The Island Horse

The
Island Horse

By Susan Hughes

Illustrations by Alicia Quist

Kids Can Press

This is a work of fiction and any resemblance of characters to persons living or
dead is purely coincidental.

Kids Can Press acknowledges the financial support of the Government of
Ontario, through the Ontario Media Development Corporation's Ontario Book
Initiative; the Ontario Arts Council; the Canada Council for the Arts; and the
Government of Canada, through the BPIDP, for our publishing activity.

Published in Canada by   Published in the U.S. by
Kids Can Press Ltd.   Kids Can Press Ltd.
25 Dockside Drive   2250 Military Road
Toronto, ON M5A 0B5   Tonawanda, NY 14150

www.kidscanpress.com

Edited by Tara Walker
Designed by Marie Bartholomew
Illustrations by Alicia Quist

This book is smyth sewn casebound.
Manufactured in Shen Zhen, Guang Dong, P.R. China,
in 10/2011 by Printplus Limited

CM 12 0 9 8 7 6 5 4 3 2 1

Library and Archives Canada Cataloguing in Publication

Hughes, Susan, 1960–
     The island horse / by Susan Hughes ; illustrations by Alicia Quist.

ISBN 978-1-55453-592-7

I. Quist, Alicia II. Title.

PS8565.U42I75 2012   jC813'.54   C2011-904470-6

Kids Can Press is a [*©*ſ*ʋ*S*™* Entertainment company

To Barb Williams,
my fellow horse-crazy childhood pal and riding
buddy; and to Sheilagh Hale, Jane Helleiner,
Beth Hunt and Miff Lysaght, wonderful
neighborhood pals who agreed to take part in so
many of our horse-obsessed activities, including
both pretending to ride *horses*
and be *horses.*

Chapter One

It was a gentle spring afternoon, and, Ellie realized with a smile, it was special.

Ellie was walking home from the village school with her best friend, Lizzie. She held her books, pencil box and slate in one arm. With her other hand, she swung her blue bonnet by its straps.

The day was special because it seemed so regular, so ordinary. The day was special because for the first time in many months, Ellie felt … happy!

The road was in front. The sea was beside. And everywhere above was the sky.

They reached Lizzie's little house. The girls were saying their good-byes when Lizzie's mother came hurrying out with a smile and a warm loaf of bread. "For you and your pa," she told Ellie.

"Thank you, Mrs. McQuarrie."

Ellie turned up the path that led to her small cottage. It was halfway up the hill from the village on the coast of Nova Scotia.

Ellie had always lived here, and she always would. It was what Ellie and her mother used to say.

"This is our lovely home." That would be Ellie's mother. She'd smile and spread her arms wide in the sunshine.

"For always," Ellie would reply.

When Ellie reached the cottage, she called, "Hello, Pa!" But this afternoon, he wasn't there. So Ellie quickly did her chores. She pumped a bucketful of water. She counted the chickens in the yard and checked for eggs in the coop. Then she cut a slice of the fresh bread and ate it while she did her schoolwork at the kitchen table.

Now, finally, she was finished her tasks. She ran to her room and got her special wooden box. She brought it back to the table. The box was full of drawings. Drawings of horses that she had done and saved. Ellie looked at her favorites. One was a horse galloping. One was a horse rearing. One was a horse stamping its foot.

Ellie loved horses, but especially horses that were wild and free. Her family had never had a horse of any kind, and neither had Lizzie's. There were a few ponies in the village, of course. But most were for pulling carts or dragging the boats up from the shore in winter. Only a few were for riding.

Ellie had never seen a wild horse. She probably never would. But she could make up stories about them, and draw them, and these were the things she liked to do most.

Ellie began drawing a horse with a long flowing

mane, standing majestically at the top of a hill. She drew on her slate, although it wasn't as nice as drawing on paper. But there wasn't much paper to spare in her home anymore. Not since her mother had gotten sick and died. Not since her father had given up his job on the docks.

Thinking of her father, Ellie looked up, and through the window she saw him. He was walking up the road in the sunshine. She could see the blue sky stretching above him. She could see the blue of the sea, the Atlantic Ocean, stretching behind him.

"Hello, my sweetpea," he said as he came in the door. But he didn't move to take off his boots. He took off his hat and held it in his hand. He stood inside the door, squeezing his hat in his fist.

In his other hand, between his fingertips, he held a single envelope. White, tissue-paper thin.

"Hello, Pa. What's that?" asked Ellie.

"A job offer, I think."

Ellie's mother had been sick for a long time, but last summer her illness had become worse. And so last summer Ellie's father had left his job. He had said, "We will spend these months together."

And they had. All the long summer, Ellie and her mother and father had stayed close. Ellie had drawn pictures for her mother and told her exciting, made-up stories about adventures with horses. When Ellie's father had cooked simple meals or hung the wash on the line, Ma sat nearby. Ma would ask to go to the top of the hill, and of course they would go. The three of them, Pa carrying Ma. They picnicked there and watched whales. They looked for orchids in the fields and made dandelion chains. They had stayed close, in their small world.

In the fall, Ellie's mother died. They buried her at the top of the hill, not far from home.

Ellie missed her mother every day. She did not want to go to school, but her father told her, "You must." And so she did, walking back and forth with Lizzie every day. And when she came home, every day, her father was there.

The long fall had passed in this way, and the winter passed just as slowly. Her father had been trying to find a new job, but could not. Times were hard. There was no paid work in the village. Those with boats fished, but her father did not have a boat. And paid work on the docks or the boats was impossible to find.

Now, Ellie's father was holding this letter. For the first time in a long time, there was hope in his voice.

Ellie waited and watched, the slate pencil between her fingers. The horse waited, its eye wild, its leg raised, unfinished.

She saw her father take a deep breath and pull a letter out of the envelope. The paper unfolded as delicately as a flower blossoming. She saw him read the letter, saw a smile split his face.

"Ellie!" he cried. He grabbed her hands and pulled her from her chair. "Ellie, we'll be all right! I *have* been offered a job. A good job!"

Ellie laughed and let herself be spun. She twirled lightly under her father's arching arms. Now maybe she could have paper for her drawings again, and her father would not be so worried. She only wished her mother was here to share the news.

Chapter Two

Later that evening, Ellie's father tucked her into
bed. She waited for him to pause before he closed
the shutters. "Good night, Ma," she whispered,
looking toward the top of the hill. It had become
her bedtime ritual.

Her father came to sit on the stool by her
bedside. The candle on her nightstand flickered.
Ellie was cozied up under an Ellie-sized quilt.
It was made of white squares edged in colors, all
sewn together. Her mother had sewn it for her,
and every night her father tucked it around her,
like a hug.

"Ellie," her father asked, "have you heard of Sable Island?"

She yawned. "Yes, Pa. We learned about it in school."

Sable Island was a small island far off their coast. It was hundreds of miles away. Forever away. In the sea. Remote and empty.

"There are wild horses on Sable Island," her father said. "Just think, Ellie. *Wild horses!*"

The horses galloped into her imagination, reared and turned, hooves flying.

Wild horses!

Ellie rubbed her eyes, and her father tucked the quilt around her again. She knew he must have mentioned Sable Island because she loved horses so much. And all night, the wild horses were in her dreams.

The next morning, Saturday, Ellie saw her father holding the paper in his hand. The job offer. He was reading it again, and then he looked up at her thoughtfully. He came to sit beside her, pulled his chair in close, put one arm across the back of her chair and rested his other hand on her knee.

"The job, Ellie," her father said. "It's a good job. But I have to tell you something. The job is on the island, Sable Island."

"Sable Island?" echoed Ellie, confused.

"I've got a shore rescue posting," he explained. Ellie didn't know what this meant, but she didn't ask because her father continued. "I'm sorry, Ellie. I'm really sorry. But we'll have to leave here. We'll have to move to Sable Island so I can work."

"Leave here?" Ellie cried. She pushed her chair away from him. She stood up. "Move? But we can't. We can't leave here, Pa. We can't leave our home!"

It wasn't possible.

"Sweetpea, I know it will be hard for you to leave here. It will be hard for both of us. But I have to take this job." Her father stood up, too. "We need it, so we can live." He hesitated. "The supply ship goes to Sable Island only a few times a year, to take provisions across and to bring back the rescued. She'll be going soon, in ten days. We'll go aboard when she leaves. That means we'll have to leave here in eight days."

Ellie stepped back. *Eight days?*

"There'll be some good things about moving to Sable Island, Ellie. Lots of good things, I hope," her father said eagerly. "We'll be given a horse so I can ride beach patrol. And then there's the wild horses. You'll get to see the wild horses on the island."

But Ellie was not listening now. His words had pushed her underwater. She could not hear and she could not breathe.

She turned and ran. She tore out of the house and up the hill. Her own steps, and her parents', had worn this narrow path. Ellie reached the top, panting. She made her way to her mother's grave.

Ellie traced her mother's name on the headstone: *Lillian.* She ran her fingertip in the carved valleys of the letters: *Wife and mother.*

It usually calmed her, but not this morning. This morning, Ellie threw herself down in the grass. She lay on her back, looking up at the blue sky, and her hands clutched the grass, not wanting to leave.

She lay there for a long time, and when the sun was straight above her, Ellie sat up. She brushed her tears away. She looked out and saw the dark blue sea. She watched the sea birds dipping and twirling above.

"Ma, we have to move. We have to move to Sable Island. But how can I leave you, Ma?" she said. "How can I?"

This was home, and nowhere else would ever be.

Chapter Three

The days passed.

Ellie could not speak. She could not eat. Still she felt as if she couldn't breathe. Still she felt as if all around her was water and she couldn't see the sky.

"Time to pack," said her father gently on the seventh day. Ellie did not have much to take with her. Just her quilt, some clothes, her pencils and slate, her school books, the precious paper she had been saving and all her horse drawings. But she had so much to leave behind. She made a list:

My ma. Visiting her at the top of the hill.

Lizzie. My best friend. We've never been apart.

Her mom, who helps us. She was my ma's friend.

My one-room school.

Mrs. James, my teacher.

The chance of a stick of hard candy. Tucked into my pocket by Mrs. Rindall in the village store.

My home. We were going to stay here for always.

The eighth day was leaving day. Ellie wakened early. As her father put the kettle on, she slipped outside. She climbed the hill before the sun was up. When she reached the top, she looked up at the dark sky and out at the dark sea. As she watched the sun rise, she knew the day was really here. Then she saw a cloud of dust coming along the road below. It was the hired cart, coming to carry them away.

Ellie stood by her mother's headstone. A fresh bouquet of orchids lay at its base. Her father had already been here this morning. She traced the words *Lillian, Wife and mother*, and said, "Good-bye, Ma."

Ellie stumbled her way down the path. Lizzie was waiting at her house. She hugged Ellie tightly and said good-bye. Lizzie's mother kissed her on the head and pressed a basket of sandwiches and cheese into her father's hands.

Ellie's father helped her up into the cart. Their few things were in back. A trunk, some chickens in a crate, several boxes and bags. Ellie gripped the sides of the cart hard, her knuckles white. Then her father climbed in beside her, and the driver, impatient, said, "Gee-up!"

Neighbors from up and down the road, and the village, too, stood near and called farewell as they rattled past. Ellie looked back. She watched until she could no longer see her house on the hill.

• • •

Two days later, Ellie and her father reached Halifax, tired and sore. It was mid-morning. Ellie stared at the rows of buildings, at the many people on the bustling streets, walking, selling, shouting. She had never felt so far from home.

They went directly to the wharf. The cart driver asked about for the schooner, the *Eagle*. It was down a ways, tied up at the farthest dock, being loaded.

"You're just in time," the captain told them. "We leave shortly."

Her father lifted their trunk, their few boxes and bundles and their crate of chickens from the wagon and paid the driver.

"Come, Ellie," her father told her. "Hurry." He took Ellie's hand, and she stepped onto the wooden gangway that bridged the dock and the *Eagle*'s deck.

The tip of her left boot was the last part of her touching home.

Ellie stood at the rail. She watched as barrels, crates and boxes were carried onto the schooner. Some lumber. A cow was hoisted aboard, eyes rolling. Last came their own possessions. For a moment, Ellie saw their chickens airborne.

The captain signaled from the wheel. The gangway was lifted. The sailors cast off the lines. They raised the sails, one fore, one aft.

Ellie's heart dissolved as the schooner slipped away from the wharf.

The wind gusted and filled the sails, and the boat plunged forward and away. Ellie looked back at the Nova Scotia coast. She watched her home disappear until all was sea. *There is nothing to look forward to*, she thought.

Ellie pulled off her blue bonnet and held it in one fist. The wind was wild. It blew her hair about her face and her skirt about her legs.

"Your first time at sea," her father said. He

stood beside her at the rail. "What do you think? Exciting, isn't it?"

Ellie couldn't smile. She couldn't even answer.

As the sun slowly rose higher, the schooner moved steadily onward. It cut through the waves, its sails billowing. It rocked, forward and aft, forward and aft.

How high is up? How deep is down? thought Ellie, lifting and sinking.

Afternoon came. Her father pointed to three whales, rising to the surface alongside the boat. Two were long and cloud gray, with bulging foreheads. One, a calf, was chocolate brown. For a time, they swam alongside, keeping pace. "They're bottlenose whales," her father told her. "Look how close they are, almost close enough to touch!"

Still Ellie couldn't smile, or even answer.

Now it was late afternoon. One of the sailors was leaning against the rails, resting. "Are we almost there?" Ellie's father asked him.

"Soon," the sailor replied curtly.

"Say, can you tell us about Sable Island?" Ellie's father asked. "Can you tell us something about the wild horses?"

The sailor scoffed. "Island!" He spat over the railing into the waves. "The place doesn't deserve the name. No trees, no rocks. It's more like a big sandbar adrift on the waves."

Ellie's father tried again. "The horses …?"

But the sailor would not be budged. He swung his arm all around, twirling his finger. "It's the wind, see? The wind is always blowing. It's moving the sand of Sable, above water and below." The sailor wiggled his fingers, making them snakelike tentacles. "Sometimes the sand spits of Sable are here." Then he flung out his other arm. It had a large hook on the end where a hand should have been. He waggled the hook. "Sometimes the sand spits are there."

He bent down and grimaced in Ellie's face. "It's dangerous. Hundreds of ships have gone aground there, on Sable. And hundreds of people have drowned there — men, women … and children." He smirked. "The island moves — here, there. Some say it's shrinking. Some say it will disappear altogether."

Ellie trembled, and her father scooped her up and away. "We've heard enough, sir," he said to the sailor, over his shoulder.

He carried Ellie along the deck to the bow of the schooner. "Did he frighten you?" he asked, holding her. "Don't worry, sweetpea. The island won't disappear altogether. Everything will be all right."

But his words did not comfort Ellie. She had lost so much already. Out here, surrounded only by sky and sea, she feared it could happen again.

Chapter Four

It was twilight. Ellie had been tired, windswept. She had sat down, wedged among some massive coils of rope at the bow, and she had fallen asleep.

Now her father was gently shaking her. "Ellie, Ellie, darling. It's Sable Island. We've arrived! Look!"

She saw the sliver of Sable Island appear out of nowhere in the dark sea. Slender and slight. A crescent floating in the blue. Almost nothing. Tantalizingly close.

They sailed on, drew nearer, and Ellie could see the shore. The surf was a white line being drawn across the beach, again and again.

The sailors furled the sails and then went no closer; the ship dropped anchor. Ellie thought, *They're acting as if the island is a wild horse, as if it can lift its head, toss its mane and whirl away. Gone.*

"Sable doesn't have a harbor where the *Eagle* can dock, so we must anchor out here," Ellie's father explained.

Ellie saw lanterns waving on the shore, many dark figures moving busily. "They'll come to get us," her father said. "Look, they're launching a smaller boat to get us and the supplies being delivered — a surfboat, small but strong and stout enough to put out into this heavy surf."

Ellie waited and watched, and now there was a small boat approaching, two men rowing it with great strength. The boat drew alongside the *Eagle*, and there were cries of welcome. Hands grabbed at lines thrown up.

Now her father was lifting Ellie, passing her over the side of the schooner. The arms of an Islander reached up from the surfboat below, caught her, held her. "Hello to you, missy, and welcome," he said. "The sea is a little rough this evening, but we'll get you landed in no time, never fear!"

But Ellie was shivering, adrift between ship and shore. The sailor with the hook muttered curses from above: "These waves want to dash us all to pieces!"

Her father lowered himself down into the boat, bringing one of their bags, and several of the sailors came aboard as well. Then the surfboat was set loose, and it lurched toward Sable, the waves high and surging.

Ellie's father held her tightly, an arm around her shoulders. The Islanders rowed, moving with the waves, trying to keep pointed toward the shore. Quickly the surfboat neared the beach, and then it surged forward at an alarming clip, sped along by the rushing urgency of a huge wave. The boat perched high on its crest, just balanced. It felt like flying, to Ellie.

The crew stopped rowing and rode the wave expertly. They were poised, alert, ready. The boat raced up onto the beach, delivered by the wave. Its bottom hit sand and skidded, spray dousing the passengers. Ellie's eyes were full of salt tears.

Immediately, before the forward momentum had even stopped, the two rowers leapt out and into the shallows, grabbing hold of the sides of the surfboat. The wave that had shot them forward onto land might drag at them, pull them back to sea in its powerful undertow. The men were digging in their heels, leaning hard toward land. Four more Islanders, ready waiting on the beach, had rushed out to help. They, too, were pulling on the surfboat, leaning, hauling again and again. Together the six men dragged the boat farther up the beach. It was as if this were a ballet and their movements had been practiced over and over.

Then there was more sand under them than water. And now, only sand. The boat was finally beyond the reach of the waves. Ellie realized that it was no use imagining they might never arrive. They were really landing.

There was a small gathering of other men on the beach, waiting with lanterns lit. They called out greetings. And then Ellie, from her seat in the boat, thought she saw someone standing alone, someone well back from the others. A woman? — no, a girl! — standing on the beach, watching. Ellie saw a blue skirt billowing like a sail. Hair whipping about. Then — did it really happen? — the girl raised her arms. Slowly she twirled away across the sand and was gone. And it was as if she had never been there at all.

Chapter Five

"Ellie, we're here," her father said, squeezing her shoulder. "We made it."

The faces around her were smiling, welcoming.

All Ellie wanted was to turn and go home. But her father's arm was around her, helping her out. So Ellie reluctantly stepped from the boat. The heel of her right boot touched the sand first. Then the heel of her left stood her on the beach.

My home is not on this island. This will never be my home.

The wind lashed her hair across her face. The sand blew into her eyes. Her tears were flying away to sea, and she tucked in her chin as she and her father walked up from the shore.

Darkness was falling. The voices of the men holding the lanterns were friendly. "How was your journey, then?" "We'll bring the rest of your things ashore in the morning." "So what's the news from over there?"

Ellie kept her eyes down.

They made their way toward a collection of buildings, the Main Station. A tall, heavyset man approached them, holding out his hand. "We're pleased you've come, Mr. Harriott. I'm Superintendent Hodgson."

Ellie's father and the man shook hands. "Call me Andrew. Pleased to be here. Thank you for the job, sir."

"Ah, you'll earn your pay, I expect!" Superintendent Hodgson chuckled.

"This is my daughter, Ellie." Ellie's father put his hands on her shoulders, squeezed them gently.

"Ah, yes." Superintendent Hodgson shifted the lantern so its light fell on Ellie. "Another young lass," he remarked.

"Young but soon to be ten," Ellie's father replied proudly.

"Well, then." Hodgson gave a quick nod. Then he swung the lantern back in front, and they walked on together.

"So, Andrew, you and your daughter will spend the night here with us at Main Station. Tomorrow Henry will take you both to Station Two. That's where you'll live. It's a fair-sized house. Two bedrooms, a large kitchen with a generous fireplace. There's a surfboat there, too, to take to rescues down your way, and a flagstaff, for signaling. We built the second station because it's impossible to patrol the whole coast of the island from one location. Here at Main Station, we're at the western tip of the island on the north shore. The second station — yours — is farther east, but not as far as the middle. We hope to have even more stations in time, still farther east."

"I see, sir," responded Ellie's father.

Ellie's head was spinning with fatigue. Her stomach grumbled with hunger as they climbed up from the beach.

"Don't worry. We're starting you slowly." The superintendent lifted his lantern high, casting a long glow. "Let you get used to the place and our ways. We still need to build a lookout tower for you there. Then we'll add some more houses. Get some more men out there, who can patrol with Station Two as their base. But all in good time, all in good time. For now, as you know, it's just you."

Ellie glanced at her father. *They would be all alone at the station?*

But her father didn't seem surprised. "Yes, sir."

"What we really need is a lighthouse," one of

the other men walking with them grumbled. "That would help save some lives, prevent some wrecks."

"Yes, well, we can dream," Hodgson allowed. He thumped his hand on Ellie's father's back. "Anyhow, here we are." They had reached the small collection of buildings. "Come down and sign some papers when you're settled."

This is the Main Station? Ellie thought with surprise. *It's far smaller than our own little village.*

The superintendent's house was two stories high, and their room was up on the second story. They pushed open the door. Two small cots. A washstand with a jug of water, a basin and a washcloth. A little window. Ellie looked out. She felt as if she was up in a tree, sitting on the branches, or perhaps at the top of a hill overlooking the sea, like the hilltop near their home …

Her father lit two candles, set down their bag.

"I'm going to sign those papers. I'll be back quick as a wink. And we'll have some supper."

Ellie wasn't hungry anymore. Just sad. And tired.

She washed her hands, neck and face. She rested the washcloth against her forehead. Sat on the edge of the cot.

There was a picture on the wall: a herd of wild horses, manes flying, facing into the wind on a sand dune.

Wild horses. There are wild horses here, Ellie remembered. *But why does that make me feel like crying?*

She closed her eyes.

A sudden knock at the door startled her. She staggered up to open it.

It was the girl from the beach. Ellie knew instantly. The same blue dress. Her hair now in untidy braids. *Oh, and she has freckles. And a pointy chin.* The girl looked about the same age as herself, maybe a little older. *She* is *real!* thought Ellie.

The girl held a tray of food and a pot of tea, leaning it against the door frame.

"Hullo. Let me come in, please," she ordered, pushing past Ellie. "This is heavy." She set the tray down with a jolt on one of the cots. The tea sloshed from the spout, splashed onto the plate of cold meat. "Oops, sorry."

Ellie stared at the girl, thinking, *There are wild horses here, and children. Or at least a girl, anyway. This girl.*

Then a voice called from below, and the girl, hearing it, raised her eyebrows and dramatically heaved a sigh. For a moment she returned Ellie's stare, and then she said, "Have you never seen a girl? Did you think there would be nothing here on Sable but seals, sand and wild horses?"

She grinned suddenly and made a silly face. "Hope you're not disappointed! Must go now, that's my mother calling." Then she stretched out her arms, one pointing ahead of her, one drifting behind. She rose up on her tiptoes, swept across the room, and was gone.

After closing the door, Ellie sat back down on the edge of the cot uncertainly. Had she just been teased or welcomed?

Before long, Ellie's father returned. They ate their supper quickly. Night had fallen now. And when Ellie fell asleep, her special quilt hugging her, she dreamed of an island girl with open arms — or was it a fairy? — and wild horses flying across the sand.

Chapter Six

It was morning, Ellie's first on Sable Island. Her father's cot was empty.

She went to the window. There was the collection of buildings they had seen last night. Now she saw outhouses and a barn. A garden. Ten or more cows and several horses in a fenced yard. Some pigs in a pen.

Near the barn, men saddled up horses, shouting good-naturedly to one another. Preparing for patrolling the beach, she guessed. On the edge of the compound, clothes were hanging on a line, flapping in the strong breeze.

There was the sea, just beyond the compound, and the *Eagle* anchored. The waves were not high this morning. Six men were hauling a wooden rescue boat out to sea through the surf. Ellie watched as they jumped in and began rowing against the incoming surge of the waves. They had to row hard to make progress. A black dog stood on the beach, barking at them.

Ellie's eye traveled back past the laundry line, across the flat expanse of nothingness, toward the tip of the island. Another two-story building was there. It was wide, with curtains hanging at every upper window, one after another, sharing a long balcony. Were they bedrooms? It looked lonely out there, and empty, too. Was it a hospital? Or maybe a home where sick people might live until they recovered?

Ellie's heart ached.

And so she looked beyond it and saw where the narrow island became narrower, sharpened to a point, like a pencil. Saw where the breakers were crashing onto the pointy tip. Beyond, the island vanished. There, the sea took over.

She didn't want to be here.

It smelled salty, like home, but the smell was stronger, as if there were more salt than air. As if there were more sea than island.

The door to their room opened, and her father came in. "Good morning, Ellie!" He joined her at the window. "How's my girl?"

She struggled to answer. She felt sadness at leaving home, but anger that her father would bring her here, to this place.

"Fine," she said, pretending, unable to look at him.

Her father stood beside her for a moment. He cleared his throat as if to speak, but then was silent. Together they looked out the window.

Then he put his arm around her shoulders, gave her a quick hug. "I've just had a short tour

42

around," he told Ellie. He pointed to one of the six small buildings clustered near them. "That's the oil house, where the oil from the seals is processed. You know, many, many seals live near Sable Island throughout the year, coming ashore once in a while. In winter, the females pup and raise their young by the hundreds, by the thousands. The men must go on sealing excursions. They hunt the seals and then cut up the fat for oil. We'll use it in our lamps."

Her father pointed at the other buildings in turn. "That's a storehouse. And those two are as well. That one is quarters for some of the men, and two families share that one."

He pointed to two buildings closer to the beach. "Boathouses." He pointed to the two-story building toward the island's tip. "Sailor's Home. Where the shipwrecked stay until they can leave on the sailing ship for Halifax."

Anger tore through Ellie. So the building

wasn't for sick people, dying people. It was for
the shipwrecked, who at least got to leave here.
"I want to leave, too!" she longed to shout at her
father. But instead she pulled away from him and
went to their bag, as if she needed something
buried deep inside.

"I've loaded our other things into a cart — it's
in the barn. Once you're dressed and we've had a
bite to eat, one of the men will take us on our way."

"All right," she mumbled.

Ellie's father waited outside as she dressed,
and then they went downstairs together to eat.
There was a long wooden table down the center
of the mess room, still cluttered with the remains
of the men's breakfast. Against the wall were a
stove with a bubbling pot and two worktables
covered with jars, breads, bowls, washbasins and
other utensils.

A woman standing at the stove turned. Over
her brown dress, with its rolled-up sleeves and

its long, full skirt, she wore a white apron with splotches of flour. Her hair, pinned up, had flour in it as well. "Good morning," she greeted them brightly. "You're the newcomers, I expect. Mr. Harriott — and Ellie, right? Come and sit down."

She was the first woman Ellie had met since leaving home, a lifetime ago. This alone seemed enough to bring back Ellie's mother to her — her laugh, her voice, her smell — and then snatch her away again.

"Morning," Ellie's father replied, smiling pleasantly. "Yes, I'm Andrew Harriott, and this is my daughter, Ellie. Pleased to meet you. Sorry to trouble you. Feeding us separate like this, when everyone else has already eaten."

"Oh, no, sit down, sit down," the woman insisted. She began ladling porridge into two bowls. "No trouble at all. It can be hard the first morning, to adjust and all." She looked at Ellie, and Ellie, avoiding her gaze, ducked her head.

"I'm Laura Chimes. I do all the cooking here."
Ellie stared at the wooden slats of the table,
unable to reply.

"Here, have some milk. And here's sugar.
There's biscuits and butter, too, if you like." Mrs.
Chimes pointed to each, set in the middle of the
table. "Help yourselves."

"Thank you, ma'am," said Ellie's father.

"Go on, then. Eat it while it's warm." As they
ate, Mrs. Chimes chatted pleasantly, chopping
vegetables and dropping them into a pot of
simmering soup. She told them about Station
Two, where they would be living. "You'll be
needing someone to help give you a hand with
things, 'til you get settled. Show you where to
look for crabs and lobsters. Show you the berry
patches — oh, we do well with strawberries,
blueberries, cranberries — how to can, how to
put in a garden. There's a bit of a garden planted
there, at your station, but it might need some

weeding." She carried a teapot to the table and poured some tea for Ellie's father, and then for Ellie. "It's a little bit of a place, our island, and there's not much that grows on sand! Not many crops, that's for certain. We can grow some timothy hay for the cattle, though. And we mow and bring in the wild hay, too."

Something caught Ellie's eye. Or was it some*one*, just beyond the mess room doorway?

"Sometimes we grow potatoes — small ones — and other root vegetables. Turnips, cabbages, red beets, corn, if they're sheltered. You'll want to do some fishing, and perhaps shoot some ducks, as well." Mrs. Chimes nodded at Ellie's father, who sipped his tea. "We have to get our flour, oats, rice and beans by schooner, when it comes!"

Suddenly Ellie glimpsed a swirl of braids. The girl pirouetted from one side of the doorway to the other. Her arms were held tight to her chest. She twirled and then was gone.

"Maybe you'll hunt seals with the men in the winter, too. You can use the oil for your lamps, you know. The extra we sell to the mainland."

Ellie's father winked at Ellie. *Is it because he's seen the twirling girl?* Ellie worried. But no, the wink was because he'd told her about the oil only this morning, she decided. *Because he wants me to feel like this is a new adventure that we are having together.*

The girl was still a secret, then, Ellie realized, pleased.

"All done, Ellie?" her father asked, rising from the table. And as Ellie got up, she now thought she saw the girl flit across the doorway again.

"Thank you for the fine breakfast, Mrs. Chimes," her father said.

"Thank you," Ellie echoed.

Mrs. Chimes stood at the stove, stirring the soup. "The two of you, living alone out there …" She paused. "Perhaps you might come in regularly, once a week or so, to have dinner with the other men. Two of them have their families here. There are five young children in all."

"We'll think about doing that," Ellie's father said agreeably. He patted Ellie's arm.

"You know, my Sarah looks to be about the same age as your Ellie — maybe a year or so older," Mrs. Chimes said, considering.

Ellie thought, *Mrs. Chimes must be the girl's mother. Hadn't the girl brought the tray last night? Sarah. Her name is Sarah, then.*

Ellie glanced toward the doorway. Nothing.

"Sarah knows every inch of this island. She was born here. She's been roaming about it ever since she could walk, ever since she could ride! It would be nice if she could show Ellie around. Perhaps show her some of her favorite secret places." Mrs. Chimes laughed lightly.

Ellie glanced toward the doorway again.

And, yes, now there was a sideways face

poking out, neck and head only. A silly face: crossed eyes, twisted mouth, tongue dangling.

Ellie almost giggled, clamping her hand over her mouth. But was Sarah making fun of her? Ellie frowned, and then the girl slipped away again behind the stairs in the hallway.

Mrs. Chimes gave the soup another stir. She smiled at Ellie and her father. "Our Sarah doesn't spend much time with the other children here. None of them are her age. She lives atop that horse of hers. Like a fairy mite, she whisks here and there, easily as you please. Never been lost or not come home, but she wanders too far." She shook her head, but spoke lovingly. "That girl of mine, she's almost like a wild thing herself sometimes."

A young man, Henry, came into the mess room, and it was time to go. "Ready, sir?" he asked Ellie's father.

They stepped out into the yard, Mrs. Chimes

wiping her hands on her apron. Now she shaded her eyes, looked about and called, "Sarah! Come here, Sarah!" But Sarah did not appear, so Mrs. Chimes went back into the house, and Henry and Ellie's father headed to the barn to get the cart. Ellie waited, seated on the back doorstep. She listened to the wind and watched the cows snatch mouthfuls of sca grass, the sun beating down on her shoulders. She heard hammering, men shouting, a dog barking.

Ellie refused to wonder about Sarah, or what living here with a mother would be like. She ran her finger across the sand at the foot of the step as if she were floating in a boat and trailing her finger in the water.

Then, *oh!* Sarah was in front of her.

Ellie caught her breath and drew back, startled.

"Hullo again," Sarah said, green eyes dancing. Freckles spread across her cheeks and speckled her nose. Brown braids reached almost down to her waist. She wore a floppy straw hat. Flower heads, yellow and white, were tucked into the belt of her blue dress, circling her waist.

"You look like a garden," Ellie wanted to tell her. But Sarah said, "Are you Ellie?" studying her.

Ellie stared back, uncomfortable. *Surely she must know my name by now.* "Yes. And you're Sarah."

The girl nodded. Her boots were dusty and scuffed. Her socks had fallen to her ankles. She flicked the ends of one braid. "You know, I've never had my hair cut," Sarah said. "Never."

Ellie said nothing.

"I guess I could show you where to look for crabs and lobsters. Show you the berry patches. We could hunt for gull eggs on the shore even."

Still, Ellie said nothing. Because maybe Sarah was just wanting to show off. Proud because she knew everything about this place, and Ellie knew nothing.

"I could even take you up the flagstaff, up to the crow's nest," Sarah offered. "You can see almost the whole island from there, on a clear day." She swept out her arm, as if willing to share the island with her.

But Ellie shook her head, though she didn't quite know why and hadn't really made up her mind. "No," she replied softly.

Just then Henry appeared from around the corner, driving a two-wheeled cart loaded with supplies and hitched to a small bay horse. Ellie was surprised by the sight of her father riding a sturdy little black horse with a brown mane. Her father! He had a happy grin on his face, looking slightly amazed himself.

"This is our new horse, Ellie," he cried. "Her name is Cora, and she doesn't seem to mind that I'm riding her. Maybe she'll be a good teacher!"

Henry pulled up and said, "Hop in, Ellie," and she climbed into the cart.

Then, suddenly remembering Sarah, Ellie turned.

Sarah had lifted her hand and was waving. "Good-bye, Ellie," she called in a friendly voice. Ellie raised her hand and gave a polite wave in return, and suddenly imagined looking for berry patches, for crabs and lobsters, for gull eggs. Maybe climbing to the top of the Main Station flagstaff. Should she agree, after all?

But Sarah sang out cheerfully again, "'Bye, Ellie," and off she ran, her braids flying, her dress billowing out, her arms wide like a seabird's.

Chapter Seven

"Gee-up!" clucked Henry. The little horse stepped forward with a shake of its head.

They left the yard and buildings, moving past a woman washing clothes in the sunlight, bending and scrubbing. Ellie watched as she dried her hands on her apron, reached down into a basket and lifted out a baby. The woman jiggled him, kissed him, plopped him back down into his nest and then returned to her work, singing.

Past the cattle. Past the flagstaff with its crow's nest, high on the hill. "We signal to ships from up there," Henry explained.

Past men, Islanders and sailors, continuing to unload provisions from the supply ship and carting them up to the Main Station.

"Food, clothing. Other things for the shipwrecked," Henry noted. "Also, building materials, new shingles — the wind is so hard on the wood! — tools, medicine, more garden seed." Ellie counted three sheep, four teakettles, two lanterns.

On they went, past the one-railed fence that tamed some of the grassy pasture beyond the station. Past the small boy swinging from the rail, his feet dangling.

And the sea was there, blue, blue. It pounded on the shore, like a drum, steady and constant. And the sky was there, blue, blue. And the wind, a painter brushing white foaming lines on the waves.

They journeyed slowly alongside the sea, along the hard-packed sand on the beach. The wind blew in from the water. It blew down from the high dunes that lined the shore. The sand lifted and swirled around Ellie, blowing into her hair, her mouth, her eyes.

Henry reached into his pocket. He passed her a handkerchief. "You might use this. For the sand. 'Til you're used to it."

Ellie held it to her mouth. She wanted to close her eyes, but her gaze was caught by the stretch of beach ribboning out in both directions, the sandy hills with their sprinkling of grass. She watched the gulls soaring, the sparrows flitting in the grasses atop the dunes. The bones of a whale, long beached. The driftwood. The timbers of a wrecked ship. "Cast ashore last night," Henry told her. "You never know what you're going to find here!"

They rode on, the wheels turning slowly in the sand. Henry and Ellie in the cart, Ellie's father staying close on his horse.

They stopped to share a jar of water, and then
Henry waved Ellie's father to lead, following
the dip in the trail. They traveled inland some.
And as the sun continued to climb, Ellie realized
she was being watched. Someone, something,
was there behind her — *is it Sarah?* She turned
quickly, and that's when she saw the wild horses.

A herd of six horses, moving across the far
dune, knee-deep in tall grass.

Two mares, each with a long-legged, knobby-
kneed newborn at her side, whisking its mop-top
tail. One yearling, prancing behind, ears tipped
forward, nickering. The stallion coming last,
pausing.

Ellie did not want to be here on Sable Island.
But her heart filled with wonder, and she stared
at him, the stallion. He, lifting his head, smelling
the air, curious, watched her.

The stallion stood, his mane lifting in the
wind, his nostrils blowing out, tossing his head.

The cart, with Ellie in it, continued on. And still the wild horse watched her. And she watched him, until he was small, smaller, and she could not see him anymore.

Time stood still. *Maybe it will be all right here after all,* Ellie thought.

But then Henry called out, "There it is! The station. Your new home, Ellie."

They drew near, and Ellie saw that it was not anything like a home. It was nothing to do with her. It was a clapboard house with sand piled up the side. It had one chimney, a rain barrel near the back steps and an outhouse some ways distant. There was a barn, a pump and a flagstaff. A surfboat with oars, for rescuing, was overturned near the beach.

This station was not on a hill. It was not between the village and the headstone of her mother. It was nowhere near Lizzie, her best friend. They might live here, she and her father, but it would only be Station Two. It would never be her home.

Henry helped them unload by the steps of the house. "Here are some stores of food. A selection from Mrs. Chimes, just to tide you over. There's a milk cow in the barn. There are some chickens already here, five or six, I think. When you're settled, you'll have to come to Main Station and get more provisions," he suggested.

Then he said farewell and was gone.

Ellie carried Cora's saddle and bridle into the barn and milked the cow, while her father watered the horse and then put her in her stall. There was a fenced yard alongside the barn with a coop, and chickens inside. Ellie and her father released their fluttery, rattled chickens from the wooden crate into this yard. Ellie scattered grain from a sack into the enclosure for them. Nearby was a grassy area marked off by a driftwood fence.

"For the cow," her father guessed.

The sun was high now, midday. Ellie's father pointed seaward. A wall of black clouds moved across the water toward them. The wind was picking up. "We'd better hurry and get our things inside," he said.

When they stepped through the door, they were directly in the kitchen.

Ellie's father grunted, setting down their trunk with a thud. Sand sifted out of its joints. Ellie set down two baskets. And then she stared. Not because the room was bare and clean, with one side table under the window, several basins and buckets and a tall wooden hutch. Not because there was a large wooden kitchen table, scrubbed and glistening, with four ladder-back chairs. But because on the table was a milk pitcher, blue like the sea and the sky. And in it were three green bowing stems with flowers atop.

One boasted quiet pink petals, lined lightly

in white. The other two waved vivid splashes of more-than-purple.

Ellie's father straightened up when he saw them. "Orchids!" He stared. "They're beautiful, your mother's favorite flower. And these two — they're her favorite color!"

"Magenta," said Ellie.

She and her mother. Looking at more-than-purple cloth in the village store. Her mother stroking it, smitten. "It has its own name: magenta."

She and her mother returning to look at it. Just to look. It is too expensive, and her mother doesn't need it. And yet, they come to look at it twice before it's sold to someone else. "Perhaps to be made into a fancy dress," her mother says, imagining it, pleased. "For a party, or a ball!"

Now Ellie's father stood in the doorway and looked at the orchids. And Ellie, remembering, looked, too.

Chapter Eight

Ellie and her father unpacked. They made up the
beds in each bedroom. They put rough towels on
the pegs, and bars of soap on their washstands.
Ellie brought in water from the rain barrel beside
the house. Some for the kitchen, some for the
bedroom basins. As they worked, her father kept
glancing out the window, looking at the sky. For a
long time, the clouds simply hung over the ocean,
angry and dark.

They unloaded the flour, raisins, butter and tea.
They found canisters for salt, soda, dried berries
and sugar. They put by the fresh cod and mackerel,

the tough vegetables and tiny potatoes of last autumn's harvest. Just before evening the rain came hard. Ellie and her father hurried to shutter the windows. The raindrops drove against the walls of the house. The wind rattled the shutters noisily.

Ellie's father made a fire and then cooked a simple meal. After they ate, they went to sleep early, again exhausted.

Next morning the sun rose, and the day was clear. Ellie padded into the drafty kitchen. Her father was finishing a stand-up breakfast. "Morning, sweetpea. Did you sleep all right?"

Ellie sat down at the table, rubbing her eyes. "Morning," she yawned.

"So, I need to tell you. I'll be away the whole day," her father said. He had cut her some slices of bread. There was jam on the table, and a pot of tea. A jar of cranberries. "I'm riding the north beach with another patroller for the first few days. We'll keep an eye out for wrecks."

Ellie watched her father's pale blue eyes sparkle in a dawn sunbeam.

"Some days I'll practice with the surfboats, practice launching them off the shore and rowing them. Other days I'll be on wrecking duty. We go aboard the wrecked ships and try to salvage any goods — barrels of salt meat, tobacco, dried cod, lemons. We have to strip the ship of its anchors and chains. Split the timbers and bring the wood ashore. We try to salvage as much as we can and store it, and then ship it to the mainland when the schooner comes. The government pays for that. It helps keep the lifesaving work here going."

He took his last bite of toast. He washed his cup and plate and set them on the towel to dry. "Sorry. I know I'm running on a bit. I know I don't quite know what I'm doing yet, or how it will really be here for us. It's just … Ellie, I think this is a good start for us. A new beginning." She looked away.

"You'll get used to it, sweetpea," her father promised. "You'll get used to it here."

He kissed the top of her head. He told her to eat. He reminded her to do her chores. Sweep the floors, tidy the rooms. Pump water, feed the chickens, check for eggs. Milk the cow and take it out to pasture.

"And don't wander far. You don't know this place yet. I'll draw you a map, in time."

Ellie hugged her knees and couldn't answer.

Long after her father left, she stared out the window. Her thoughts were a storm inside her head.

She went to her room, got dressed and made her bed. She drank a few sips of cold tea. She looked at the bread her father had cut for her, the wooden table, the milk jug. The orchids.

She went outside. She might almost be interested in exploring, except that she didn't want to be here. There was nothing but grass and sand.

Remembering her chores, she pumped water and carried the buckets indoors. She scattered some feed for the chickens and checked for eggs. None. She milked the cow and left the bucket in the cool of the barn, putting a towel over it to keep the flies off. She led the cow outside to its patch of grass.

The wind blew. It swept through the yard, swirling sand into Ellie's eyes.

Grass and sand. No trees. Not one. *It's obviously not an island made for people,* Ellie grumbled to herself, rubbing her eyes. *Look at this house!* She thought it must have been made on the mainland, nailed together into sections, then loaded up and brought over, piece by piece.

And the barn. She stared at it, folding her arms. *It looks as if it's been made with timbers from wrecked ships.*

A few gulls wheeled, making dipping shadows

in the yard. Ellie's shadow angled out in front of her. Tall. Alone.

She stretched out her arms. Turned them this way and that, making dipping shadows, too. And then, without deciding to, she began walking. She walked so she wouldn't have to stay in any one place. So she would not have to be here.

She turned her back on the house and the sea and walked inland, scrambling through grasses and wild hay. She lifted her feet up and away from this thin slice of accidental land. The seagulls floated overhead. The sparrows darted here and there. The wind was always behind her, around her.

Ellie walked into nothingness. She didn't recall her father's warning about wandering. There was emptiness all around her and inside her.

Nothing matters, she thought. *It doesn't matter if the sand shifts. It doesn't matter if the whole island dissolves away into the sea.* This was not her home. She was not here.

Tiring, she headed back to the beach, her shadow on one side, the sun on the other.

Ellie walked beside the sea until her legs grew weary. She had reached a stretch of dunes that rose abruptly right near the edge of the beach, high beyond the water's reach. She sat down in the long marram grass at the foot of the dunes. And then, exhausted, she lay back and fell asleep.

Waking, she had sand in her eyes, and the straps of her bonnet were twisted under her chin. She pulled at them, cranky, loosening the knot. Her skirt had ridden up from her boots. Her shins were hot in the spring sunshine.

Ellie lay, looking at the sky, and suddenly, she saw the horse.

She gasped and almost cried out in surprise.

He was there. It was the same stallion she had seen yesterday. She was certain of it. The horse was only several arm-lengths away, grazing. He was above her, near the top of the dune, silhouetted against the blue sky, and she gazed up at him from where she lay.

The horse was stocky with a shaggy coat. Ellie felt him close, his body real and sudden. Would he hurt her? Was he dangerous?

He's wild! A wild horse! she told herself, unbelieving.

Chewing, the horse swung his head round. He looked down at Ellie. His brown coat was the color of milk chocolate. His mane was black and very long. It lay along his neck in waves. His forelock fell between two watchful brown-black eyes. A sweep of the wind lifted the forelock to one side of his face, revealing a patch of white on his forehead. A thin white stripe ran down his nose.

He blinked, and his long black eyelashes waved. Ellie held her breath. She was awestruck, captivated.

For a long moment, Ellie stared into the horse's soft, curious eyes. Then she thought,

He's so close, I could touch him. He would feel warm, soft. As velvety as orchid petals. He seems so calm, so tame. He wouldn't hurt me. Should I? Should I reach out and ...

Ellie lifted her hand. She was still only thinking about touching the horse. But he understood her instantly, before she even knew her own mind.

The wild horse jerked his head up and whirled. He would *not* be touched!

He was so close to her that she felt the stir of the air as he pirouetted. She felt the sand from his hooves spray her bare shins.

The stallion pounded away over the dune, knees high and sand flying. Then he was gone.

Chapter Nine

The next morning while they ate, Ellie's father described Cora to her. "Our horse is very gentle and sweet, Ellie. She's also very patient. She's a fine little horse" — he chuckled — "which is lucky because it's up to her to teach *me* how to ride! I bet she could teach you, too." He looked at her tentatively. "If you'd like to try her sometime, on one of my days off maybe …?"

Ellie shook her head. "No." She could not imagine it. "No, thank you, Pa."

"Ellie, she's from here, the island. She was once wild."

She shook her head again.

Ellie knew wild. She had seen wild yesterday, the horse on the dunes. What was "once wild" compared to that?

When they were finished eating, her father drew her a map on her slate.

"This is Sable Island," he said, drawing a crescent moon, thin at the ends, slightly thicker in the middle. "It's about twenty-five miles from tip to tip, and only one mile wide at its widest point." He made an N above the middle of the moon's smile. "That's north, and here we are." He put an X between the middle of the moon and the western end.

"And here," he marked an X on the north shore at the western end, "is the Main Station, where we landed and slept on our first night." He moved his finger back to the X that was their station. He ran it a little farther along the coast and then down, inland. "The salty lake, Lake

Wallace, stretches from here," he ran his finger eastward, "to here. It's long and skinny like the island itself."

Ellie was interested, trying to calculate the place on this map where she had seen the horse.

"Ellie." Her father spoke sternly, waiting to get her attention. "It's a small island, but in a fog or a storm you could get lost. If you ever do," he said firmly, "stay in one place. Don't move, and I'll come and find you."

He waited.

"All right, Pa," Ellie agreed.

And suddenly sadness swept over her, because she felt lost now, here. In this new place.

Her father left for his beach patrol, and Ellie remained at the kitchen table, still feeling adrift and alone.

Then into her imagination, behind her closed eyes, came the wild horses. They found her!

Ellie erased the map on her slate and drew

them: the stallion standing on a dune, its mane long and flowing. Then one mare pawing in the sand for water. Then the little ones. Then, after one more erasing, the rest of the herd so close they were overlapping, no space between them.

A ray of sunlight slanted across the wooden tabletop, rested on the orchid petals. Ellie put more water into the jug. Gently, she touched her fingertip to the pink and white blooms, to the magenta.

She thought of the stallion, real and wild. He might be there! And she hurried to get dressed.

Just as she was leaving, she remembered her chores. Quickly, Ellie washed the dishes and dried them. She laced up her boots, hurried to the barn, milked the cow and took it out to pasture. She threw handfuls of grain to the fowl. She ducked into the hutch, ignoring the clucking and the ruffling of indignant feathers. One egg. No, two, three. She cradled them in her skirt, grabbed the pailful of milk and returned to the house. She placed the eggs in a bowl on the wooden table and covered them with a wet cloth. The milk, too.

Now Ellie was ready. She grabbed up her bonnet and walked out. She moved quickly eastward across the sand. The wind was whooshing, pushing the waves into frothy tips, dashing them against the beach, as regular as breathing. In and out, in and out.

Sandpipers scurried along before her. Plovers with a band of black feathers around their necks fished in the shallows. Ellie found part of an oar washed up on the shore and, farther along, a coconut, bald and foreign. She walked around them, warily.

Just as her legs were getting weary, Ellie reached the dunes. There was no sign of the horse. So she sat and waited.

Ellie looked out at the blue ocean, the diving terns. She waited there, and the wind blew gently.

The sand wafted between the grass, over her, about her, into her hair, her eyes. She could taste it on her lips. Sand and the saltiness of the sea that the wind shared as well.

She gazed sleepily at the sand at the base of the dunes. There were tiny circles in the sand, perfect circles, millions of them.

The fairies have come, she thought. *The fairies have danced here in tiny circles.* The idea slipped in and out of her imagination. So did the memory of Sarah, pirouetting, twirling. Suddenly Ellie longed to tell someone about the fairy circles, but there was no one to tell.

A sparrow flitted through the grasses, then took flight. The sun was high now. The clouds that had been far off were closer. Ellie tilted the brow of her bonnet to keep the heat from her face. She took out an apple from her pocket.

Then Ellie caught her breath. It was the stallion. He came over the dune, and here he was, so close to her, only a few pirouettes away.

When he saw her, he stopped, but he did not seem afraid. He tossed his head and snorted, his nostrils flaring, and Ellie held in a giggle.

The stallion bent his long neck. His black forelock fell over one eye. He grazed, tugging at the marram grass, yanking it up, chewing it, swallowing. He pawed at the sand, and ate more grass.

She gazed at him, letting her eyes rest gently here, there. The muscles in his shoulder rippled as he stepped closer, grazing. His black tail twitched. His mane lifted in a sudden gust.

Without thinking, Ellie lifted her hand, palm out. She presented the apple to the horse.

He lifted his head. He stepped forward, stepped again. Gently he breathed on her hand, nostrils flaring. Then delicately, he took the apple, his velvety lips brushing her skin. He crunched, jaws grinding.

When he was done, he looked at her, and
Ellie held her breath. She dared to meet his gaze.
Stared into his brown-black wild eyes.

Neither of them moved. Ellie did not even blink.

They looked at one another, and Ellie knew
he saw her. Saw her here, in this place, in this
very moment.

And she had never felt so alive, with her feet
on the sand, and the wind in her hair, and the sun
on her skin. She was alive, here and now. And so
was the horse. They were here together.

Chapter Ten

Ellie sat with the horse, watching him, memorizing him. While he ate, while he dozed, while he ate again, she decided on a name for him: Orchid. The hours passed. And still she sat and watched.

Then something shifted. She felt the air change and get cooler. She shivered. And she saw the horse had wisps of mist snaking through his legs, over his withers, under his belly.

Is it fog? she wondered, and almost as she thought it, the horse seemed to vanish.

Ellie could not see a thing. She could not tell if the horse was still there. She waited, hoping he might come close, press his muzzle against her. She did not want to be without him.

But he was wild, and he had gone. And when she finally got up and stood, wanting to leave, even the dunes were gone, and the sea. The fog was all around her.

Ellie shivered again in the damp air. The wind had picked up.

How will I find my way? she wondered.

Ellie felt a flash of fear. She stood uncertainly. She tried to remember what her father had told her, just that morning. *If you get lost ...* but her thoughts were skittery, scattering. She had that underwater feeling, like she could not see, could not breathe.

Just then, it seemed to her that suddenly something was near. Not the horse. Something else. A fairy perhaps?

No, something much larger. And there it was. A huge, dark shape, moving in the fog, quite close, uttering a reedy "Hullo." But what could be so big and have such a high, sweet voice?

"Hello," Ellie replied, startled.

The shape came closer, and then the bridled head of a horse emerged from the fog. A hand reached down, a person — *of course!* — atop.

"Come on. I'll take you home. Here, use my stirrup." Scrambling up onto the back of the horse, she knew it was Sarah. The girl's hair was braided, and she wore a blue dress, and that was all Ellie could see through the fog, even though they were now front to back on the horse. "Right. Here we go."

They moved through the fog, traveling along the shore, only seeing where they were just as they got there. Ellie caught another glimpse of Sarah and discovered that she wasn't wearing a blue dress, but rather a blue shirt and brown breeches, and she sighed aloud, longingly, "Oh, breeches. You're lucky."

"I guess," Sarah agreed, then gave a delighted laugh, as if just realizing that other girls might not be allowed this freedom.

Riding in the fog felt like floating. Like bobbing along on a boat at night. Like swaying amid a cloud, out of time. Like living on this island.

Sarah tipped her head back toward her. Ellie saw a flash of her pixie-sharp chin. "My horse's name is Shannon," she said.

The fog began to lift from below, so that beneath their thighs the island was reappearing. Ellie saw Sarah's feet, bare in the stirrups. She saw the horse's hooves. A chain of wildflowers around Shannon's right front fetlock. Tiny petals, glistening with fog droplets.

"How did you happen to come upon me? In all that fog?" Ellie asked.

"I was coming to visit you," Sarah replied easily. "I came yesterday morning, but you weren't at the house. So I rode up the beach, but by the time I spotted you by the dunes, the sun was high and Ma needed me back home to help out. And to work on my lessons. Today I came again. I rode up the coast for a while and looked for seals. Saw lots on the beach!" she said enthusiastically. "I was coming to visit you when the fog came in. I thought you might be there again, by the dunes, and not find your way back. I wasn't far away, so I came."

Sarah came yesterday and was watching me? And again today? Ellie gasped. *Oh, no! Did she see my horse? My secret island horse?*

"You've been spying on me!" Ellie burst out angrily. "Spying!"

Sarah's back stiffened. Her chin rose. She didn't speak.

The girls rode on in silence.

When they got to the station, Ellie slid down until her feet touched the ground. She knew she must say thank-you. She thought she could manage it once there was more space between her and the wild spying girl. But once Ellie was off the horse, Sarah and Shannon were gone, vanished into the fog, into the wind, into the air.

Chapter Eleven

The next day, the morning sky was dark and cloudy. The wind was high.

Ellie was slow getting up. It seemed like night. She yawned, stretched and dozed.

Her father knocked gently on her bedroom door. He poked his head in. "It's a fierce day," he warned her. "Stay inside."

She wanted to roll over. She wanted to pull up the bedcovers and go back to sleep where everything could be as she wished. But something pulled at her. Something would not let her fall back into that deep place.

Ellie got up. She dressed and ate, listening to the wind rattle the windows. She did her chores. Found four eggs. Swept the kitchen floor. Made the beds. Even baked a simple cake for supper, remembering to keep the fire low and even, like her father had shown her. Then, the kitchen warm with the smell of cooked apples, she knew she should sit and draw, or talk to the cow in the barn, or look out to sea from her bedroom window. After all, her father had told her to stay indoors. But it was also her father who had brought her to this nowhere island in the first place. Her thoughts kept returning to the dunes. Orchid might be there!

She remembered to close the shutters. She put on her sweater, her waterproof slicker over top and her boots. Then she set out along the beach.

The ocean waves were high and rolling. They broke on the shore wildly. Her hair whipped her face. She was nervous.

She kept walking. Once she turned, feeling as if perhaps she was being followed. But there was nothing behind her. No one.

She thought about Sarah. Ellie had been so upset imagining that Sarah was spying on her. She wanted Orchid to be her secret, her one good thing in this empty place. *But maybe I was too harsh,* she thought. *If Sarah did see me with Orchid, maybe she didn't tell anyone. Maybe she understands. Maybe she just wants to be friends, after all.*

Ellie reached the place where the dunes came right to the edge of the beach. Orchid was not there.

She waited, crouching, then sitting. Knees pulled up to her chin. The grass bent around her. The sand was damp. The sky was threatening. The horse was not there.

An island of sand. What if the wind blew it all away? What if we're left without anything? Ellie wondered.

The storm hit. The rain came suddenly, and the wind drowned out all other sounds.

Ellie sprang up, covering her head with her hood. Discouraged and disappointed, she peered into the distance, inland. No horses were there. She looked along the shore. No horses here either, although there were seals. They had hauled out along the beach. Gray seals. Dozens of them. They lay on the sand as if they had always been there and would never move. As gray as the air, as the rain-filled skies.

Hunched, holding her elbows, Ellie turned quickly back toward the station. She walked briskly along the dunes, drenched. She kept her head down, the rain blowing at her from the ocean side. She thought about her father's warning with a flush of shame. Thunder made her jump. Her heart was pounding.

The wind picked up even more, and the rain fell harder, pocking the sand. She felt the whole island shudder, as if it might simply dissolve into grains and vanish.

There were no trees, nothing to protect her from the opening skies. And then a lightning bolt lit up the horizon. Instantly she saw it, in the sea, as she turned to sweep the wet hair from her face. A ship! It was offshore and tilting at an impossible angle. Its sails flapped uselessly.

It wasn't moving. It had hit ground, slammed into a sandbar. Ellie imagined the sailor with the snaking fingers, remembered his frightening words.

She heard cries carried in the wind. *Is it the crew?* she wondered. *The passengers? How many are on board?* She watched in horror as the waves crashed up and onto the ship's deck.

Ellie saw two figures on horseback. They were riding along the shore, galloping from the west toward the ship. They skidded to a halt and gestured to one another. She could hear them shouting. *Is one my pa?* she wondered, but they were too far away to see, and the rain was like a curtain.

One rider lit his lantern, waving it toward the ship. It would tell the passengers that help was on its way. It would bring hope to the shipwrecked.

The other rider had spun about, galloping along the beach and then turning, veering inland. He must be going to get the others, Ellie decided, heart pounding. The rider bent forward, low over the horse's neck, lifting in his stirrups as the horse's pumping legs drove them up the side of the dune. The horse and rider crested, and then they were gone.

Was that my pa? Or is this him on the shore?

Ellie stood waiting, watching, as the ship tipped and tilted. Maybe it would ride out the storm. Maybe it would not sink further.

Minutes passed. Her knees gave out, weary with terror, and she sank down on the wet sand.

She clutched the hood at her neck, shivering in the rain, and waited for help to come.

What was taking so long? Where were the men, the lifesavers?

The man waiting on the shore sat astride his horse, huddled, a wet sentinel.

The sea was alive, the waves beating the shore so that the island shook again and again. The ship rocked dreadfully. The waves continued to crash over the ship's deck.

More lightning, and now Ellie thought she could see people on board — the crew? passengers? — clinging to the rail. The ship was not far away, but the water looked deep. No one could get to shore from there without knowing how to swim, and even then … She remembered the waves hurling them from the *Eagle* to shore, and she shuddered.

Ellie swept her hair back. Water ran down her face as if she were weeping. She put her hands over her ears. The sound of the wind was too much. The sight of the ship was too much.

I should leave here. I don't want to be here. The words pounded in her head.

But then, suddenly, there was someone beside her. A small shape in a wet raincoat, with braids poking out the front of the hood. Sarah had come over the dunes. In the raging wind, Ellie had not heard her. Ellie saw Sarah's horse, Shannon. The horse waited, head bowed in the rain, reins dangling in the sand.

"A rescue," Sarah cried, raising her voice to be heard. She was not making silly faces now. Her brow was furrowed, her eyes worried. Ellie nodded back. Sarah sank to her knees in the wet sand beside her, and Ellie felt good not to be alone.

There were two horses coming along the shore, shoulder to shoulder, their heads bobbing, their knees high. They were pulling something that Ellie couldn't see through the pounding rain.

There was a man beside them, gripping the bridle of one. He was bent forward, leaning, as if pulling the horses.

The waiting man leapt from his horse and ran to meet him.

Through the gray sheet of rain, Ellie glimpsed a wooden boat emerging from behind the pair of horses. It looked heavy and moved clumsily through the sand. It was a surfboat, perhaps the one from their beach. There were five men alongside the boat as well, pulling.

Ellie clasped her hands together. They would rescue the people on board! No one would drown, she decided. The ship was wrecked, but the people would be saved!

The girls stared together at the boat on the beach, at the ship, then back to the beach. Ellie strained to identify the shoremen. The men were urging the horses forward, closer to the water's edge. The man holding the bridle gestured, and two of the men began detaching the boat from the harness. It was done quickly, and the man moved the horses away.

Sarah leaned close and shouted, "Is your father there?"

"I don't know. I can't tell," Ellie yelled back. "Is yours?"

Sarah didn't respond, seeming not to hear.

The six men held the rescue boat, three on each side. Its bow was in the water. The waves crashed over and into it. There was a yell, and they all began hauling forward, bending like trees falling. They went out to their knees, their thighs. One wave, two, three.

Then suddenly, all the men leapt aboard, and quickly each grabbed an oar. Straightaway they began to row.

"Pull!" Sarah burst out. "Go on, pull!" Her arms were wrapped tightly around her legs. Her fists were clenched.

The men pulled on the oars, and, unaware, Ellie leaned with them, bending in time with each stroke. The surfboat began to head offshore slightly.

But the waves and the wind were fierce. They pushed back at the small boat.

The men hauled on the oars again, straining incredibly. Ellie held her breath. The shoremen fought to get beyond the shallows. The surf was breaking over the bow, soaking the oarsmen, filling the vessel with water.

It was dangerous. The surfboat might capsize.

What if my father vanished into the sea? Ellie wondered with a shudder. *What if he slips away from me, too?*

She could not stay, but she could not go. She could not watch, but she could not tear her eyes away.

The surfboat was slammed head-on by one huge wave. The shoremen's oars beat against the sky and could not get purchase. Ellie cried out. The boat was bucking on the crest, as if it were a wild horse and the men were riding it.

The wave shot the boat back toward the shore. One man, letting go of his oar, fell out over the side, and was catapulted onto the beach. He struggled to his feet. The water was only knee-deep, and though the waves rushing back out to sea sucked at him, pulling him in, he staggered to shore.

Another wave, even larger than the last, carried the boat right back onto the beach, tossing it onto the packed sand like flotsam.

The remaining men jumped out. Four of them grabbed the sides, intending to try again. But the fifth man, at the bow, shook his head no and waved his arms. He must have been the captain of this patrol, for the others obeyed without protest. It was clear the sea was too fierce, the surfboat was no match for it.

The men, defeated, could only pull the boat farther up onto the beach, then stare through the pelting rain at the tilting vessel and wait.

Finally, Sarah spoke. "Come, Ellie," she said. "Come. We need to go."

Ellie was shaking so hard she could barely straighten her knees, her spine. She could hardly lift her head. She was cold. Water streamed down her face.

"Come, Ellie," Sarah repeated. And Ellie let Sarah help her onto the horse, Shannon. Sarah climbed up and slipped in front of her. Shannon's flanks were wet, but their warmth told Ellie how cold she was. Ellie could not stop shaking. Sarah reached for her hands and placed them on her slim hips, saying, "Hold on to me, Ellie. Don't fall off."

When they reached the second station and Ellie saw their clapboard house, relief welled up in her.

She slid from the horse, her soaked skirt clinging to her legs.

She stood in the rain, looking down at her boots, at Shannon's black hooves, and said to Sarah, "Thank you."

And then she repeated it louder, above the sound of the rain and the wind, and the beating of her heart.

Ellie didn't know why Sarah would be so generous, so forgiving, but the freckled girl said, "Ellie, if you ever need me, fly a white flag on your flagstaff, and I'll come."

Ellie lifted her face, the rain falling full onto it. Sarah grinned and made a silly face. Then she turned her horse, twirling Shannon like a fairy might on a fairy steed, and off she flew.

Chapter Twelve

Ellie's father was seated at the kitchen table, buttering his toast. The worst of the storm had passed. Now, this morning, sunlight was spilling through the windows. It touched the pot of tea, turning it a soft yellow.

Ellie reached out her hand. She slid it into the sunshine, across the wood of the tabletop to the warmth and light.

Her father had not returned until very late last night. Ellie had eaten alone. She had made a small fire in the fireplace, curled up in her quilt on a chair and waited.

When she wakened, she found herself wrapped tightly in her father's arms. He was carrying her to bed. His hair was wet, his face exhausted but happy. "Pa," she breathed in relief.

He told her of the ship run aground on the shoal, the crew aboard. He described the first rescue attempt, the desperate rowing and the failure to break free of the beach.

Gently, he had settled Ellie into her bed and tucked the covers around her. "But we saved them," he had continued. "We waited for hours until the wind and the surf died down and the heavy rain let up. Then our men got the surfboat off the beach and out to the ship, and they brought all seven crew ashore. All seven! Saved!" Sitting on the side of her bed in the darkness, he laughed with relief.

"I only waited ashore," he explained, "showing our light to the ship. Trying to give them hope that we wouldn't abandon them. I'm not experienced enough to help with the surfboat yet."

Ellie hesitated. She was, of course, filled with relief that all the men had been saved. She was also overcome by a fierce happiness as she realized that her father had not been in danger. But there was another feeling as well that surprised her. "Pa, you did well," she said softly, proudly.

Today, her father had the day off. They did the chores together. Then her father boosted her up onto Cora and swung himself up into the saddle in front of Ellie. "Just hold onto me, sweetpea," he instructed. "Don't worry, we'll go slowly!"

The sky was clear, and one of the other patrolmen, Ross, was taking them fishing on Lake Wallace. Her father explained that the lake was brackish, neither freshwater nor seawater, but something in between. Fierce storms caused ocean surges, the water rushing over the island beach and into the low-lying lake. The wild horses would not drink this water, Ellie knew.

"We have to head inland," her father told her, and they turned their backs on the sea and rode with the sun on their left.

At first, there was sand underfoot. Then it turned to scrub and tough short grass. They could no longer hear the sound of the surf swooshing on the beach. The wind was not so fierce today.

"They tell me that Sable Island is one of the windiest places in the whole country. Because of the wind, and the sea salt, too, trees can't grow here, and plants don't grow very tall. This place might almost blow away." Her father said it without a trace of fear, incredulous, marveling. But Ellie pictured floating on a bar of sand, adrift. She shivered.

"Except for the marram grass," he told her reassuringly. "That's marram grass." They were riding along the edge of a dune, and her father pointed to the tall grass growing there. Then he surprised Ellie by halting Cora and jumping off.

"Here, look!" he cried. He grabbed some of the grass and pulled and pulled. But he couldn't yank it out. "See? See how tough it is? The roots of this grass grab onto the sand, deep, deep down. There's nothing there to hold onto, but they do anyway." He patted Cora's neck and picked up the reins. "The grass holds on and won't let go, and this lets the dunes form. The grass keeps them intact. There aren't any dunes to protect Lake Wallace. But the dunes protect the island's two or three freshwater ponds from the salty seawater. The horses need those ponds to survive." He smiled at Ellie. "This grass won't let the island blow away, Ellie. It's tough!"

Ellie sat alone on Cora's back, uncertainly.

"Here, Ellie, scoot forward and sit in the saddle," her father suggested, helping her.

He began walking, leading the little horse. "Hold Cora's mane if you like," he suggested. "That'll keep you steady."

After a time, to her surprise, Ellie felt safe.

The island stretched on either side of them. Now, for the first time in days, Ellie could not see the ocean at all. She was without it.

"Ellie, look. There'll be berries here," her father said, pointing. Tiny buds decorated low spindly branches on bushes. "Look at all these! This is a place to remember."

Ellie imagined the bushes bursting with red, blue, purple. She thought of Sarah. Before she could push the thought aside, it came: *Will Sarah and I come berry picking together here?*

Then, she asked the question she had been harboring since yesterday afternoon. "Was Sarah's father there last night, too?" she asked her father. "At the rescue?"

Her father walked on in silence for a moment. Cora's saddle creaked. A gull screeched overhead, soaring.

"No, sweetpea. Sarah's father is dead," Ellie's

father finally said. He patted Cora's neck as he walked. He didn't look back at Ellie. "One of the other men told me that he drowned on a rescue two or three years ago. But this island is now Sarah's home, and her ma's. So Sarah's ma stayed on here as cook."

Ellie's eyes filled with unwanted tears.

This island is not a home, she thought fiercely. *It's just sand. Some buildings on sand. A place to get shipwrecked. A place to rescue others from. A place to leave.*

Chapter Thirteen

Up they went, over a rise. Ellie's eyes opened wide. A thin lake like a pointed finger stretched out before her, so far that she wasn't sure whether she could see either end. Lake Wallace.

Lush green plants and clusters of white flowers bordered the water. Four mallard ducks slept, their heads under their wings. A flock of sparrows chattered at the edge of the lake, then rose as one.

Near the shore was a burly, busy man, Ross. He was loading fishing gear into a small sailing boat. He saw them approaching, smiled and called, "Hallo, Andrew! And you must be Ellie. All set for some fishing?"

Her father greeted the man, and quickly they hitched Cora on a long lead to a nearby bush. They got into the craft and pushed off.

Ellie pushed her bonnet back and let it dangle from its straps. She unbuttoned her sweater. The sun felt good.

The white sail billowed out, and the boat shot forward. They seemed to race across the water.

Ross talked as he held the lines. "In the summer, Wallace is sometimes only half a mile long. But in the winter, when storm waves flood the lake, it can stretch for many miles," he boasted. He told them lurid stories of hurricanes, shipwrecks and drownings.

Ross tacked the boat back and forth across the narrow lake. The wind here was fine, manageable. Ellie trailed her hand over the side of the boat, feeling the warmth of the water. She gazed at the shore, her thoughts turning to Orchid. *He wouldn't bring his herd here to drink. But would they come to graze along the shore?* she wondered suddenly. Ellie sat up, scanning the shoreline carefully.

Nothing. The sailboat skimmed on across the water.

But then, when she had almost given up, Ellie caught sight of a group of small figures in the distance, on the crest of a small rise. She looked intently. Horses! Wild horses! She counted. Four adult horses, and three small ones, the foals. It was not Orchid's herd. There were seven, not six, and Orchid was not there. Yet they were lovely all the same.

Ellie turned to share this small gift with her father. But they had reached a curve in the lake. Ross was dropping the sail, and Ellie's father watched, eager to help. Ellie could not catch his eye.

"We'll try for flatfish here," Ross said, anchoring.

"All right," her father agreed cheerfully.

"Want to have a try?" Ross asked Ellie.

"No, thank you," she replied politely, then turned back to watch the horses. But already they were leaving, moving over the rise and out of sight.

"Maybe next time," said Ross with a shrug, and he baited two hooks.

The boat bobbed on the water, and Ross talked even more as he and Ellie's father fished. He told them about the history of Sable Island. How it had been sinking ships for hundreds of years. How it sat astride the great route that the sailing ships traveled from the east coast of North America to Europe. How it was known as the Graveyard of the Atlantic.

"The first lifesaving station was put here in 1801," he said. "I've been here myself for fifteen years, and I've seen many a poor fellow drown. We need more than the one main life station here. We've got the second station now. Your station." *Ours?* thought Ellie uncomfortably. It didn't feel like theirs. It couldn't be her home. Not ever. "But we need a few more," added Ross. "And we need some better lifeboats. And a lighthouse."

Ellie's father nodded, jerking his line.

"It would help prevent some of the tragedies," Ross said. "We do our best, with our dozen and a half men or so and our two surfboats, but it's a dangerous place, and it's taken many lives …"

Ross reeled in his line. There was a fish on the end, struggling. "Here we go!" he grinned, pleased. "A nice flounder!"

"Tell us about the wild horses," Ellie's father suggested. His hook was empty. He rebaited with another small mud minnow, and tossed it back in.

Ross turned to Ellie. "Have you spotted any of them, the wild horses?"

Ellie hesitated. But Ross did not wait for a response. "Well, they eat hearty all spring and summer, so they can make it through the winter. In the cold season, they have the dried-up marram grass to eat, and they have to break the ice on the ponds with their hooves in order to drink. But their shaggy winter coats and their long manes keep them warm." He gripped the fish's flapping body and took the hook from its mouth. "They're used to people, somewhat. You can *look* at the horses. But you can't get too close. They're just too wild."

Ellie smiled to herself. She recalled Orchid's breath on her hand, his lips brushing her skin.

Ross slapped one hand on his knee. "Say, if you're interested in the horses, you'll want to come to the roundup. It's in three days' time. This Saturday. It's always quite an event. Have you heard about it? We chase the herds of horses across the island," he said excitedly. Ross made a rough circle with his arms. "Chase them toward the corrals that we set up." The fish continued to flop in his grip.

A roundup? Ellie's throat tightened. Ross began closing the circle of his arms, like a noose, as he explained, "We corral as many of them as we can. We might catch twenty or thirty."

Ellie saw it. She could see the whites of the eyes of the wild horses. Their tails lifted high. Shaking their heads angrily.

"Then we choose the best ones. We take them to the seashore, and we tie them down, kicking and screaming. Then we lash the horses to something like a stretcher, and we get them to the surfboat, load them up two or three at a time. Out they go to the *Eagle,* where they're hoisted aboard with ropes." Ross gestured, making a scooping motion with one arm.

Ellie saw the kicking hooves, the horses screaming for help. She saw the heavy bodies airborne. They were swinging over the water, rolling eyes wide and white. "The other horses in the corral we let go. But those ones — the best — we ship to the mainland. They can fetch a good price there. The funds help to pay for running the station."

Finally, Ross threw the fish into the bucket. It flopped about among their other catches of the day.

Ellie's stomach lurched. She saw the shiny flat bodies of the fish twitching. Their eyes stared. Their gills flapped. Caught.

Ross and her father turned to talk about other things, eel spearing on the lake by lantern light. "Eels make a good stew," said Ross.

But Ellie wasn't listening. She was imagining her island horse chased, thrown, tied. She imagined him unable to rear, to turn and gallop away, sand flying. Then, worst of all, she imagined Orchid being shipped away. She imagined him being shipped away from his island home.

Chapter Fourteen

What should I do? What can *I do?* worried Ellie.

It was the next morning, Thursday, and Ellie was hurrying to the dunes.

She hoped to see Orchid. Her heart ached to see him. She was starting to love him. She couldn't help it, even though she knew she shouldn't. Because what if she loved him, and he was captured in the roundup and lost to her forever?

Ellie reached the dunes by the shore. She climbed to the top, and she sat and waited.

The horse arrived before too long. This time

he trotted up from behind her. Her heart jumped when she knew he was there. He stopped in front of her, stood and looked at her. Still, he was not afraid.

He grazed near her feet. He came so close.

Maybe I should leap on his back and ride him, she thought crazily. *Capture him. Throw a rope around his neck. Put him in the barn at the second station. Hide him.*

The roundup was in two days.

Ellie stared at him, his long mane, his thick chocolatey-brown coat like velvet. Orchid tugged at the tough grass. The muscles in his powerful neck flexed. He chewed, his jaw sliding from side to side. He was a Sable Island horse, tough as the marram grass but as beautiful as the orchids she and her father had received on their first day here.

She whispered it to him. "You are as beautiful as orchids."

The horse's lashes lifted, and he gazed at Ellie.

She stared back into his eyes. Again, a moment of wonder, fragile and delicate.

Ellie heard a neigh in the distance. Instantly, the horse's head turned, and his ears flicked forward, searching.

She turned and saw them, across the dunes. Finally! Orchid's herd. Her heart caught in her mouth. Five horses. Five oh-so-beautiful horses. The same ones she had seen on her very first day here.

One was the smallish yearling with a chestnut coat, likely born the previous spring. It sprang about on strong legs, nipping at its mother's flank, wanting to play, or maybe just dance.

The two mares were also the color of chestnuts, their coats a glossy tangle. Some of their long winter coats remained, and were dropping.

The two foals tripped along behind them. They were tiny. *So tiny!* marveled Ellie. But sturdy. Their tails were short little whisks that flicked, flicked, flicked. The foals were chocolatey-brown, the color a mirror of their father's coat. And they had his markings, too. The white patch on his forehead, the thin white stripe down his nose, his dark mane and tail. *They are his little ones all right,* Ellie thought with a grin. *This is his herd.*

The foals waited. Flick, flick. The mares waited, too, and the yearling. Patient. Bending their heads down to snatch a mouthful of grass. They would wait forever if they had to. They were his herd.

The stallion tossed his head. He snorted. *Whuff.* And he cantered over to join them.

Ellie smiled again and wrapped her arms around her knees. She settled in to watch Orchid and his family. She would happily watch forever, if she could.

Chapter Fifteen

Later, back at the station, Ellie's happiness was chased away by worries about the roundup. Ellie couldn't think of anything else. At dinner, she saw horses being pursued and corralled. As she tried to sleep that night, she saw horses being roped and lifted. The horses shrieking, kicking. The horses leaving the island forever.

Ellie knew she had to do something to prevent Orchid from being captured, hoisted onto a boat and shipped to the mainland. Maybe his mares were at risk, too. Maybe the yearling, the foals even. Ellie had to help. But how? What could she do?

On Friday morning, she looked at her father as he sipped his tea. He was leaving for patrol duty soon. Perhaps he could help, somehow.

But what if I tell Pa and he won't believe me? Won't believe I have a secret friendship with a wild island horse? she worried. *Or what if he doesn't want to help?* Can't *help? What if he has to join in the roundup and help capture Orchid? What if it's part of his job?*

And there was something else preventing her from telling. There was something fragile between her and the horse, something impossible. Ross had said, "You can't get too close. They're just too wild." Yet fear had not come between Orchid and her, the fear a wild horse might feel for a human. Orchid had come to trust her, and she him. Whatever it was connecting them seemed reliable. Safe. But if Ellie told, the telling might change that. The fragile something might break. And she would lose him.

So Ellie let her father go out on patrol and didn't say a word about the horse.

She wondered if Sarah would come that day. Sarah had offered help. "If you ever need me," she had said, "fly a white flag." Maybe Sarah would come and Ellie could find a way to talk to her about Orchid. Even though Ellie wasn't certain about Sarah yet, time was running out. The roundup was tomorrow.

But the day passed, and Sarah did not come.

Then it was Friday night. Ellie went to bed and closed her eyes, and she saw it all again: Orchid being chased and corralled. Being roped and lifted, shrieking and kicking. Leaving forever. Leaving her, leaving his home, his herd.

"Pa?"

She found him in the kitchen. The fire had almost died down. He looked up at her and smiled, stretching his arms. "Just about to turn in," he said. "Everything all right?"

"Pa, there's a horse, a wild horse …" she began.

Ellie's father wrapped her special quilt around her, and settled her in a chair. He stirred up the fire. The wood blazed, then steadied. He pulled up a seat next to Ellie and listened.

She told him about the island horse, and what he meant to her. She described seeing him for the first time. About how she had visited him several times. She reminded him of what Ross had told them, about the roundup.

Ellie talked, and her father listened closely.

Finally she dipped her head, and her hands were dashed with tears. "I'm afraid. The stallion is in danger, Pa. And maybe his herd as well."

Her father was careful and calm, and he didn't hesitate. He said quietly, "I'll help you, Ellie. I'm not sure yet what I can do, but of course I'll help you." He pulled his chair even closer to hers. He tucked the quilt around her snugly. "Now, let's just get comfortable here. I'll need to think for a while."

Ellie lifted her face to him at once. Her eyes, full of hope, searched his. She saw he would do anything for her. Then she rested her head on his arm, and they sat together. Ellie watched the fire dance. She watched as the fire burned low.

Then Ellie, half-waking, felt her father lifting her, carrying her to bed.

In the morning, Ellie started awake. *It's Saturday!* she thought in alarm. She ran to her father's bedroom, saw the empty bed and hurried to the kitchen. A lantern was lit. The sun was just rising.

Ellie's father was standing at the table, drinking a cup of tea. "Ellie," he said, upon seeing her, as if there had been no sleep, no night in between their last shared words. "I've only been able to come up with a simple plan. I've thought long and hard, and this is all I have come up with." He shook his head. "I don't think we can appeal to the other men. I don't think that would work."

Ellie nodded. She knew he was right.

"So here it is. I agree your horse is in danger —
likely not the yearling or the foals, but possibly
the mares, because they could be broken to ride
or to pull a wagon." He paused. "Do you think
you could drive the stallion, gently, or somehow
lead him? Take a rope, maybe, and lead him,
and perhaps the herd might follow?" Her father
was looking at her hopefully. "Ellie, could you
try? Because it's all I can think of. If you could
head east with the horse, you could go to the
sand hills." He took her slate from the table and
quickly drew another map of the island.

"Here we are, here." He pointed. "And here,
past the end of Lake Wallace, eastward along the
south shore, are the sand hills. They're isolated.
Just off the beach. Out of the way. I think if you
tried to go there with the horse, you might be
able to hide him and the rest of the herd among
these big dunes."

He made a semicircle with his fingertip around the area. "The roundup doesn't begin until midday. I'll head over to join the men now. Eat lunch with them at Main Station. And then I'll try to steer them away from those hills, move them to the west, north or east of there," he promised. "I don't know how I'll do it. They'll expect me to follow along, it being my first time. I'll have to think of something. Fall off Cora. Play the fool." He smiled and shrugged. "Pretend to know things I don't."

Ellie listened intently as her father spoke. Her heart filled. He would do this for her!

"It's all I can think of," he apologized, but it was everything to Ellie.

Her father finished his tea, and then, as he rose, the sun's first rays slanted across the sea. He buttered some bread, took it in his hand and hurried to the door. "Good-bye, Ellie. Good luck," he cried. "Be careful no one sees you along the way!"

"All right, Pa," she agreed. "Thank you!"

He gave a wave. She watched by the window as he saddled up Cora, and she watched as he galloped away to join the roundup riders. Ellie wanted to hug him. With all her heart, she wished she had hugged him. But he was gone.

Chapter Sixteen

Ellie quickly went and got dressed. She wasn't
hungry, but she knew she would be out all day.
She cut two slices of bread and buttered them.
She slipped the buttered bread into her pocket,
for later, along with several slices of cheese, an
apple and a jar of cold tea. Then she put on her
boots and her sweater, and she hurried outside.
Quickly she milked the cow and fed the chickens.
The other chores could wait.

She was about to head to the sand dunes, to
Orchid, when she saw the flagstaff there, tall. Silent.

She heard Sarah's words again: "Ellie, if you

ever need me, fly a white flag on your flagstaff, and I'll come."

Oh, I need her now. I need her very much, Ellie knew.

She raced back into the house to her bedroom. She grabbed her special white quilt, and was rushing through the kitchen when she saw the orchids on the table. Pink and magenta.

Ellie was holding the quilt her mother had made for her, and there were the orchids that her mother would never see, and she was remembering the magenta that was her mother's favorite color. She had lost her mother and her home. Was she going to lose her island horse as well?

She was underwater, she couldn't breathe, she couldn't speak. Ellie pressed her face into the quilt and missed her mother, for always.

But then, as she stood in the kitchen, and it seemed to her that the waves were crashing over her and she was sure she was drowning, suddenly she heard the wind blowing again, and she felt the sun shining. She went to the window and watched the waves washing against the sands of the island, and she knew the wild horse was on the dunes. His head held high, his mane waving in the wind. He was waiting.

Her father was out there, too, trying to help. And Sarah … Maybe Sarah would come!

She felt herself floating to the surface, and she gulped in air, big breaths, because now she could breathe, and maybe she was all right. Maybe everything would be all right.

She needed to help the island horse. She needed to hurry. Ellie flung open the door and raced to the flagstaff with her quilt.

There was a rope on the flagstaff with loops and toggles. Quickly, she attached the quilt, tying the ends through the loops, struggling to tighten them, working as fast as she could. She pulled hard on the ends so that she was certain it would not fly away, into the wild, wild wind. The quilt was secure.

And then she pulled on the rope. Hoisting her special flag, the white squares with the beautiful colored edges. She pulled and pulled, and up, up it went, to the very top of the pole.

Ellie tied off the rope, stepped back and looked.

The quilt unfurled. The wind caught at it. Pulled on it, opened it out. It flapped in the wild wind, signaling for help.

"I love you, Ma!" Ellie shouted the words into the wind, seeing the quilt flying. "I'll love you for always, wherever I am!"

Ellie turned and ran along the beach, pleading fiercely, "Sarah, please see the flag. Please come."

She needed to get to Orchid. She needed to find him. Her feet dug into the sand. The wind blew against her. The waves pounded in her ears, and so did her heartbeat. She panted as she ran, and ran, and ran.

Ellie reached the dunes and collapsed, gasping. She waited and hoped. Would the island horse come to her this morning? He had to. *He had to!* She didn't dare to think that he might not.

Ellie waited, and time passed, slowly, slowly. The wind continued to blow, and the sun began to rise higher in the sky. She knew that at midday the riders could come, hooves pounding, cries ringing out, to chase Orchid and his herd, to corral them.

The horse did not come.

And still, the horse did not come.

But then Ellie heard a sound behind her, the sound of hooves, galloping. Her heart leaping, she turned.

It wasn't Orchid, but it was Sarah!

"Ellie, Ellie! I saw your signal!" Sarah called, slowing her horse. Shannon tossed her head, pranced. "What is it? Is something wrong?"

Ellie sprang up and ran to Shannon's side.

"Sarah, it's roundup day!"

"I know," said Sarah.

"Sarah, the horse … my island horse … You saw me with him, that first time you came to visit, and then that second time, before the fog …" Ellie's voice faltered.

Sarah laughed. "The day I was spying on you?" she teased. Then, more seriously, she went on, "No, Ellie, I didn't see a horse. What horse do you mean?"

Ellie blushed. So Sarah *hadn't* been spying, *hadn't* seen Orchid, and she'd accused her …

"Ellie, quickly, you must tell me. What island horse? One of the wild ones?" Sarah asked urgently.

"Yes, a wild stallion, Orchid. I've named him Orchid," she confided. "Oh, Sarah, I'm so sorry I said you were spying. I'm so scared for Orchid and his herd." It all came out in a rush. "Sarah, I have to save them." The wind blew Ellie's skirt about her legs. She paused, then asked, "Will you help me?"

Sarah answered at once. "Yes, of course. Of course! What do you want me to do?"

Ellie swallowed. "I'm not sure," she said. "My father has gone to join the roundup riders. Somehow he's going to try to lead them away from the sand hills near the south shore, at the eastern end of the island. I'm hoping Orchid and his herd show up here this morning, soon. Then," she paused, almost not believing it herself, "I'm going to try to take them there, to hide among the sand hills."

Sarah's face was serious. She chewed on her lip as she listened. "All right. That sounds like a good plan, Ellie." She nodded.

Ellie's heart beat quickly. *Sarah thinks this might work! She thinks we might be able to save Orchid and his family!*

"So, maybe I should do something like your father, try to keep the roundup riders away from that section of beach." She was asking Ellie, but

Ellie saw that she was also deciding to do it as she spoke. Sarah was already urging her horse away, grinning over her shoulder. "Shannon and I will come up with some good ways to distract them. Don't worry, Ellie. I think we'll be good at this!"

"Thank you, Sarah! Thank you," cried Ellie.

And Sarah was on her way, with a wave of her hand, a twirl of her wrist. Shannon was cantering, digging up the sand with her hooves that were ringed in flowered bracelets.

Ellie took a deep breath, feeling fear and excitement, and also, now, a tiny stirring of hope.

Things seemed better. Sarah had come to help, even though Ellie had not been very friendly to her so far, and Ellie wondered if maybe Sarah understood something about what it was like to be adrift. Maybe, like the wild horse, Sarah could see to the heart of things, see into Ellie's heart.

Chapter Seventeen

Ellie sat down again on the dunes and waited for the horse. She waited and waited. She tried to be patient. She tried to be calm. It was all she could do.

She looked up. A tern darted across the sky, wings bent. Another followed. The sleek birds were white, their heads capped with black. Wings folded, one plunged into the ocean. Ellie saw the bird rise and dart away, a fish in its bill.

She breathed slowly, trying to remain patient.

"Where are you?" she whispered into the wind. "Why don't you come?" As soon as Orchid came, they would need to leave. The trek to the sand hills would take some time. It would be best to be there, hidden, before the roundup started. If they were found on their way …

"Where are you?" she whispered again.

Ellie closed her eyes. She counted to one hundred.

She opened her eyes. Still no horse.

She closed her eyes again. She counted to two hundred.

"Please be here. Please be here."

She opened her eyes.

And there he was.

The island horse was moving over the crest of the dune. She saw that he was looking for her. His head lifted up high, and he found her.

His herd was not with him, but Orchid was here! Tears of relief came to Ellie's eyes. Like a sunshower, she was smiling and weeping.

But the roundup riders could come whooping over the hill at any moment.

She had to take him, move him. She knew that she couldn't put a rope on him, couldn't ride or guide him with a halter. He was a wild horse. He would always be wild. But there had to be a way.

Ellie turned and looked toward the east. She would try to lead him along the coast, and then cut overland past Lake Wallace to the south beach, then eastward again to the sand hills. She looked back at Orchid and realized he was watching her.

Ellie took a few steps toward the east. Then she took a few more steps, slowly. As if the wind would always blow, and the waves would always wash against the sand, and all the time was now.

Would the horse follow? Would he come, because it was her, because he would want to be near her?

Orchid bent his head and grazed. He bobbed his head, seeing her go. He snatched more grass, and chewed.

Pausing, Ellie held her breath.

The horse looked up at her again. He took a few steps, and then a few more, toward her.

Ellie's heart raced.

She waited a moment, and then she walked a few more steps along the dunes. Then she took a few more steps.

The horse bobbed his head again. Again, he snatched a mouthful of grass. Again, he followed.

"There are wild horses on this island," her father had told her, and it was true. It made her heart sing.

Ellie walked east, along the crest of the dunes, toward safety. Orchid followed closely.

They walked on, she ahead, he behind.

And after a time, she realized that they were not alone. She turned her head slowly. The herd was there! The island horse's little family. Two mares, the yearling, the two foals.

She saw them coming from the west, following along the crest of the dune.

They were following their stallion, their leader.

They did not come close. Sometimes they were out of sight, in a valley or hollow, as Ellie and the island horse topped and descended a low rise, or when lingering to graze. Or even, once, when the littlest foal lay down, its tiny, knobbly legs giving out abruptly.

But Orchid seemed unconcerned. He seemed certain of their loyalty and their bond to him. He came forward after Ellie and put them in her care as well, trustingly. Sometimes he stopped to drink or to rub his leg daintily with his muzzle. And sometimes he was so close she felt his breath on her shoulder or her arm.

The wind blew, and the waves surged against the shoreline. It was a day like every other on the island — wind, waves and sand. And yet today Ellie was walking with her horse, and she had never had such a feeling of happiness bursting inside her chest.

Chapter Eighteen

The morning turned into afternoon.

We're moving too slowly. The roundup will be starting soon, Ellie fretted. *Maybe it's started already!*

Ellie had never been this far along the island before. After walking eastward for some time, she had turned inland, found Lake Wallace and walked until reaching its eastern end. And all the while, she had worried that the roundup riders would come bursting upon them, hallooing and whooping, and sweep her little brood away.

But they hadn't, and she and the horses had

kept walking, moving southward. Now they had reached the southern beach and were moving eastward again. They should come upon the sand hills soon. *Soon,* Ellie hoped.

She was getting tired. She walked with her head down, determined. Trying to keep the pace brisk.

As long as the roundup riders don't come ... as long as they don't find us now ... she told herself over and over.

Suddenly, from atop a high ridge of sand, as she glanced out along the coast, searching for the hills, she saw strange tall bones rising in the distance. Astonished, she saw them sticking out of the beach, an enormous rib cage.

What?! What strange animal is this? Could there be more, still roaming the shores? Ellie wondered fearfully.

She shuddered, but she had nowhere to go but forward. She drew closer, along the ridge, her heart thumping. But as she came near, she realized, with relief, that the bones were not bones. Rather, they were the wooden skeleton of a wrecked ship. They were timbers, stripped to white by wind and waves.

Ellie's legs were weak from worry and her hours of trudging. She paused to scan the horizon again, looking for the hills. Her stomach grumbled. Realizing she was famished, she hastily ate a piece of cheese and drank a few sips of cold tea.

There was no time to waste, however, so she walked on, and the horses followed. And then, as the sun had reached its summit and was dropping lower, into mid-afternoon, she stopped and looked ahead again, shading her eyes. Ellie saw shapes in the distance that looked like mounds, rising from the beach.

There they were! The sand hills! Finally!

She picked up her pace. Orchid and his family stayed near.

But then, glancing back at him, always watchful, she saw his ears prick up.

"Oh, no," she cried because she, too, thought she heard something in the distance, approaching. The roundup riders? Was it them? She wanted to cry, to give up.

The stallion raised his head higher, listening. He halted.

Ellie stopped, too. She wanted to sink down, drown.

Then Orchid turned his head, and looked at her. Fear and surprise were in his eyes … Was he going to panic? Flee toward danger?

She couldn't let it happen.

"No, we have to hurry. We have to hurry! Come on!" she called. She would not let them find him. She would not.

Ellie started to run. She summoned up all her energy and her hope and her love for the island horse, and she started to run as fast as she could.

She ran toward the hills, and when she glanced back she saw Orchid duck his head and kick up his heels. Then he tossed his mane and reared, and now he was galloping after her.

He caught up to her and continued on past her. He raced along the sand, tail high, hooves pounding. And now *he* was the leader. He was guiding Ellie, urging *her* onward.

She ran after him, as hard as she could, buoyant, and behind came his little herd, trotting, anxious to keep up.

As if they were all connected by an invisible thread, the stallion tore across the sand, exuberant and full of life, with Ellie and his family following.

And they reached the sand hills. Orchid disappeared behind one hill, and the other horses disappeared after him. Ellie stopped running, stood panting. From where she was, from where any roundup riders might be, the herd could not be seen.

It was late afternoon. But they were here, and no one had found them. Maybe it would be all right.

Ellie walked in among the sand hills, found Orchid and sat down gratefully. The horse stayed nearby, eyeing her. Was he wondering if there might be another exhilarating tear across the sand? He tossed his head and pawed his hoof in the sand, restless.

But after a time, the stallion settled. And he did not leave, although there was little food here, no grass at all. He dug down in the sand, and then drank the water that appeared. One by one, first the foals, then the yearling and then the mares came and drank. And then Ellie, watching and thirsty, went to the hole Orchid had made, and cupped her palm. Drank the fresh water.

Satisfied, she sat back on her heels and wiped her mouth with the back of her hand. Then she gasped.

Orchid was there. Right there, next to her.

She sat still.

Slowly, the horse stretched out his neck toward Ellie. He looked at her carefully. Then he hesitated.

Ellie held her breath.

Orchid's ears twitched. His muzzle came close. She felt his nose touch her shoulder, her elbow. He pushed at her gently. His nostrils flared.

Ellie remained still. She dared not move.

Yet now he was nudging her palm. Once, twice. She felt his velvety nose on her bare skin.

And so, slowly, slowly, she lifted her hand. She stroked his nose with the tip of her fingers. Once. Twice.

Ellie looked into Orchid's deep brown black eyes, and he gazed back.

It was a moment only. But it was everything to Ellie.

Then, with a snort, Orchid stepped away.

He tossed his head, and he flicked his tail. He headed back to stand near his herd.

Now it was early evening. The sun was still in the sky, but it was low. The rays were sliding across the sea toward them. The horses were here. They were together, with her.

Ellie, strong and determined, knew that no matter what happened, even if the roundup riders came and found them, she would protect the horse. She would not let him be taken. She and her father, and Sarah, would save Orchid and his family, too. Together they would not let the horses be taken from their home.

Chapter Nineteen

Ellie awoke in her father's arms. A crescent moon was shining down on a crescent island.

"Ellie, I found you," he breathed. "You made it here!"

"It's over?" she asked, although she knew it had to be, because it was night.

He nodded. "Yes, sweetpea. The roundup ended long before the sun went down. They corralled sixteen horses in all. But it's over now."

Ellie felt a pang. Sixteen wild horses had been taken. She knew some would be set free. Only the finest would be shipped away. But still …

Her father asked anxiously, "And your horse …?" He lifted his head and looked around. "Is he here? Is he safe?"

Ellie looked around, too. She saw sand and sea, and moonlight. But the wild horse had gone. And the others, too.

"He's not here anymore." Ellie smiled at her father reassuringly. "But he came with me. He followed me here, away from the roundup. And his little herd came with us. I know he wasn't taken."

"So, he's safe. And his family as well."

"Yes, they're all safe," Ellie said. "Thank you, Pa, for helping."

"Oh Ellie, you're welcome, but I didn't actually do much!" he said lightly. "After lunch, we all headed out. I managed to tag along with two fellows who were heading this way. Although they seemed quite sure none of the stallions had claimed these sand hills as their territory, it was their job — *our* job — to check."

He chuckled. "Well, I was able to delay them along the way. Poor Cora! I fell off her twice, no, three times! The first two times, she looked surprised. The last time, she actually looked a bit sorry for me!" He chuckled again. Ellie grinned, picturing it.

"And the lads weren't angry at all. Just laughed at me and said I needed riding lessons. Then finally they said we should turn back or we'd miss the roundup completely. So we never made it all the way out here, in the end," her father concluded.

Ellie turned her head and pressed it against her father's chest. She hugged him. He had made himself look foolish in front of these men just to help her. "Thank you, Pa."

"You know, I think it's that lass Sarah you need to be thanking," he said, hugging her back. "I heard she created quite a commotion in the middle of the afternoon. She raced out to the riders moving east with some strange story. Told them they were needed back at the Main Station right away. That the *Ellie* needed help."

Ellie caught her breath in surprise. But her father laughed — "The *Ellie!*" — and Ellie, relieved, laughed with him.

"They all turned back right away. Almost came the whole way in before they got wind that she was leading them in a dance." Her father shook his head, smiling. "She's quite a one, that Sarah!"

Ellie swallowed hard. Sarah had done all this for her! For her and Orchid and his herd.

She hugged her father again, and he held her more tightly. She almost couldn't believe it. Orchid and his family were safe. There would be another roundup sometime. Maybe next year. Maybe sooner. But Orchid and his family were safe for now, and to Ellie, tonight, this seemed enough. More than enough! It was wonderful.

And I'm *safe.* Ellie felt it suddenly. She knew it.

I'm safe. Even here, on this island. Maybe especially here, she thought, thinking of her father, Sarah, Orchid.

Her father stood up, still holding Ellie in his arms. "Time to go home, sweetpea," he said.

Ellie's father lifted her up onto Cora's back. Then he mounted, sitting behind the saddle, wrapping his arms around her.

Tomorrow, she would tell her father about naming the horse Orchid. She would tell him all about Sarah. And she would tell him that she'd like to continue her reading, writing and arithmetic. *Maybe I could have lessons with Sarah,* she thought. She imagined it for a moment and grinned. *It would be fun!*

But that would all be tomorrow.

Now, Ellie closed her eyes and leaned back sleepily against her father. They set out, making their way across the shifting, moonlit sand. Together, she and her father were going home.

Author's Note

If you went back in time to when this story is
set, in the early 1800s, you would not have had
the pleasure of meeting Ellie or her father or
Sarah. All the characters in *The Island Horse*
are invented. They came from my imagination.
However, the characters did grow out of real
places and real situations, and I have based many
of the details in my story on historical fact. Take
Sable Island itself. This magical place actually
exists. Look at any detailed map of Canada and
you can pick out the tiny crescent-shaped island

lying about 160 kilometers (100 miles) off the coast of Nova Scotia.

It really is mostly sand and vegetation. There is only one tree on the whole island. And the island does grow and shrink in size over time. Storms, tides, currents and waves shift and shape its edges. As I write this, the island is approximately 40 kilometers (25 miles) long and about 1.5 kilometers (one mile) at its widest. But if you checked today, its measurements might be different.

And what a dangerous place it was for ships. Sable Island sits on a rich fishing ground and near a major shipping route. But it is often covered in fog, it is frequently hit by storms and there are unpredictable currents surrounding it. In the past, navigational tools were not always good enough to help sailors safely make their way around this treacherous location. That is why there were many, many shipwrecks near the island. In fact, there have been more than 350 recorded shipwrecks there since 1583. The island deserved its nickname, the Graveyard of the Atlantic.

Also, there really was a lifesaving station on Sable Island. The first one was built there in 1801. Crews of men came to live and work on the island. They looked for shipwrecks during storms or foggy weather. They tried to rescue any survivors who were aboard. They also searched for shipwreck survivors who had come ashore. It was a hard life. But over time, the men began bringing their families to live on the island. For example, the first superintendent, who arrived on Sable Island in 1801, brought with him his wife, his children and several staff members.

So it is likely that if a man such as Ellie's father got a job on Sable Island, he would have brought his daughter along with him as well. It would have taken them more than one day to sail to Sable Island from Halifax, but they would certainly have traveled there on the supply ship. And yes, a shore rescuer would have patrolled the coastline on the back of a Sable Island horse, since it is also true that wild horses have lived on this Canadian island for hundreds of years.

How did they get there? No one knows for certain, but the first horses probably arrived in the early 1700s. They were domestic or tame. Some say they were shipwrecked there. Others say they were shipped from the mainland to the island because it was a place where they could graze freely. However, over time the horses returned to being wild, living a natural life and moving in small herds.

Just as in this story, some of the wild horses were regularly rounded up and sold in Halifax once or twice a year. This happened for decades, well up until the 1950s. Usually they were used for pulling wagons or riding. Then, in 1960, a federal government department thought the horses were starving. It decided to remove them all from the island and auction them off for dog food or glue. Shocked Canadians, including many children, wrote letters to Prime Minister John Diefenbaker to protest. Shortly afterward, a law was enacted to protect the wild horses.

And now there are other laws, too, to protect the island and its horses. For example, no one can go there without written permission. No one can feed or interfere with the horses. Although scientists and researchers come to study the island's unique wildlife and fragile habitat, no one lives on the island anymore. There are also hopes that, one day soon, this island may become a national wildlife preserve or park.

Since I was a child, I have loved horses. And since I first read about Sable Island, this special home to wild horses, I have dreamed about setting a story there. When Ellie spoke to me in my imagination one day, it was time to create my own Island Horse world, made of fact, fiction and dreams. I am so happy to have shared it with you!